Gossie

Olivier Dunrea

Houghton Mifflin Company Boston 2002

For Ed

www.houghtonmifflinbooks.com

The text of this book is set in 20-point Shannon.
The illustrations are ink and watercolor on paper.

Library of Congress Cataloging-in-Publication Data
Dunrea, Olivier.
Gossie / written and illustrated by Olivier Dunrea.
p. cm.
Summary: Gossie is a gosling who likes to wear bright red boots every day, no matter what she is doing, and so she is heartbroken the day the boots are missing and she can't find them anywhere.
ISBN 0-618-17674-8
[1. Geese—Fiction. 2. Boots—Fiction.] I. Title.
PZ7.D922 Go 2002   [E]—dc21   2002000214

Manufactured in China
SCP 10 9 8 7 6 5 4 3 2 1

This is Gossie.
Gossie is a gosling.

A small, yellow gosling who
likes to wear bright red boots.

Every day.

She wears them
when she eats.

She wears them
when she sleeps.

She wears them when she rides.

She wears them when she hides.

But what Gossie *really* loves
is to wear her bright red boots
when she goes for walks.

Every day.

She walks backward.

She walks forward.

She walks uphill.

She walks downhill.

She walks in the rain.

She walks in the snow.

Gossie loves to wear
her bright red boots!

Every day.

One morning Gossie could
not find her bright red boots.

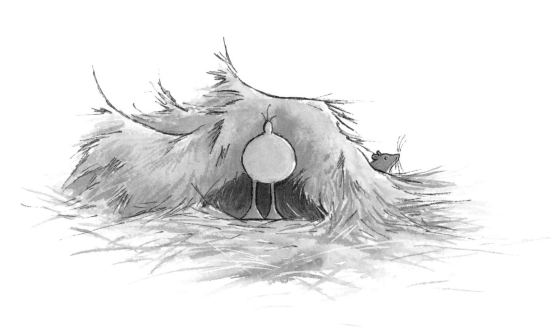

She looked everywhere.
Under the bed.

Over the wall.

In the barn.

Under the hens.

Gossie looked and looked
for her bright red boots.

They were gone.
Gossie was heartbroken.

Then she saw them.

They were walking.

On someone else's feet!

"Great boots!" said Gertie.
Gossie smiled.

Gossie is a gosling.
A small, yellow gosling who
likes to wear bright red boots.

Almost every day.